TREE SOLDIER

Abram,
To remind you that
what really counts
~is enjoying the
people who love
you ~not things!
All my ♡
GramE

Written by Sarah M. Flores

Illustrated by Maksym Stasiuk

For Makena

In his regular house, on his regular bed,
sat a boy named Billy, scratching his head.
"I'm bored with my toys. I'm bored with my games.
I'd be happy if Mom and Dad bought me more things.

My house isn't fun. It's small, and so old.
I wish it was a castle, with floors made of gold."
Billy grabbed his red jacket and his new tennis shoes.
He'd go for a walk and find something to do.

He stepped out the door; the sun was bright in the sky.
Trees lined the road, protecting homes nearby.
The trees were green, giant, sturdy, and straight.
They guarded homes like nature's gate.

Billy leaned on a tree and took a break from his walk.
The tree wiggled, and shook, and started to talk!
"Grrreetings, young fellow, it's sure nice to meet you.
I'm Tree Soldier. How-do-you-do?"

A talking tree? Billy put his hand on his head.

Was this real, or was he dreaming in bed?

Tree Soldier wiggled his trunk and he rustled his leaves.

"Billy, grab hold of my branch. Take a walk with me!"

Billy and Tree Soldier marched down the road.
They stopped at a house that was one to behold.
Billy peeked over the fence and admired its size.
It was a mansion, with a pool, and a tall, curvy slide!

"Their house is huge," Billy said, "with so many rooms.
There's games, and toys, and a big swimming pool!
They must be so rich! They must be so glad!
They can play in their house and never be sad."

Tree Soldier gathered Billy in his branchy arms,
then placed him in the family's yard.
Billy looked through the windows, surprised by the sight
Tree Soldier grinned, "Is everything all right?"

"The parents aren't talking. The girl is on her phone.
The boy is playing a video game, but he's still all alone.
They're all by themselves in the same room,
but there's so many things this family could do!"

Billy looked at Tree Soldier for an explanation,
and Tree Soldier replied without hesitation.
"They have a big home, nice cars, and nice things,
but that doesn't make them a happy family."

Tree Soldier bent down and took Billy by the hand.

"Join me on this journey, and you will understand."

Tree Soldier wiggled his trunk and he rustled his leaves.

"Billy, grab hold of my branch. Take a walk with me!"

Billy and Tree Soldier marched down the road.
They stopped at a house that was tattered and old.
Billy peeked over the fence; he could barely see the house
It was oh-so-very small—small enough for a mouse.

"This house is so little. There's only one room.
It needs new paint, and a mop, and a broom.
They don't have much money. They must be so sad.
I'll bet they're bored, irritated, or mad."

Tree Soldier gathered Billy in his branchy arms,
then placed him in the family's yard.
Billy looked through the windows, surprised by the sight.
Tree Soldier grinned, "Is everything all right?"

"The dad is cleaning and cooking dinner on the stove.
The mom is sewing something—I think it's baby clothes.
The sister is reading a funny story to her brother.
He's smiling, and happy, and ready for another."

Billy looked at Tree Soldier for an explanation,
and Tree Soldier replied without hesitation.
"Their house might be small without many things,
but they're still a loving and happy family."

Tree Soldier bent down and took Billy by the hand.
"Join me on this journey, and you will understand.
Next, we're going to a house with few things . . . or a lot.
Inside there lives a boy who's sad . . . or maybe he is not."

Billy and Tree Soldier marched back up the road.
"That's my family!" said Billy. "That's my home!"
"You said you were bored with your family and things.
How about now? Has anything changed?"

"My little brother's running, and he's pulling a red wagon!
My sister's chasing after him, pretending she's a dragon!
My mom is laughing loudly, and she's clapping, too.
My dad is pretending he's a bouncing kangaroo!"

Billy nodded at Tree Soldier and smiled with great cheer.

He had something to say . . . it was suddenly clear.

"Who cares if a house is big, medium, or small?

What matters most is what's inside . . .

. . . the love you have for all."

Made in the USA
San Bernardino, CA
13 May 2018